CAROLINE BINCH has illustrated children's books for Rosa Guy,
Oralee Watcher and Grace Nichols as well as writing and illustrating
a number of her own titles. Her illustrations for Rita Phillips Mitchell's
Hue Boy and *Down by the River* were shortlisted for the Kate Greenaway
Medal in 1993 and 1996, with *Hue Boy* going on to win the Smarties Prize.
Caroline is perhaps best known for illustrating Mary Hoffman's bestselling
picture-books *Amazing Grace*, which was shortlisted for the Kate Greenaway
Medal, *Grace & Family* and the story book *Starring Grace,* all published
by Frances Lincoln. Her other Frances Lincoln titles are *Gregory Cool*,
shortlisted for the 1995 Sheffield Libraries Book Award, the Nottinghamshire
Libraries Book Award and the Kate Greenaway Medal, *Since Dad Left*,
winner of the United Kingdom Book Award in 1998, Kathy Henderson's
New Born, and *Silver Shoes,* shortlisted for the Kate Greenaway Medal
and the Sheffield Libraries Book Award in 2002.

For Amy and Kingfisher Blue

Silver Shoes copyright © Frances Lincoln Limited 2005
Text and illustrations copyright © Caroline Binch 2001

First published in Great Britain in 2001 by DK Publishing, Inc.

First paperback edition published in Great Britain in 2005
by Frances Lincoln Children's Books, 4 Torriano Mews,
Torriano Avenue, London NW5 2RZ
www.franceslincoln.com

British Library Cataloguing in Publication Data available on request

ISBN 978-1-84507-471-5

Printed in Singapore

3 5 7 9 8 6 4 2

Silver Shoes

Caroline Binch

F

FRANCES LINCOLN
CHILDREN'S BOOKS

Gran's bottom drawer seemed like a treasure chest to Molly.
Inside were sparkly bags, shiny shoes, and brightly coloured shawls.
Beautiful things for Gran to wear when she went dancing
with Grandad.

"Can I wear your silver shoes, Gran?" Molly always asked.
Clickerty-clackerty went the heels as Molly danced.
She felt just like a grown-up lady.

At home, Molly danced with her best friend Beverly.
They liked to dress up and copy the pop stars on television.
"Girls, I think it's time you went to dancing lessons,"
laughed Molly's mum.
"Can I have some silver shoes?" asked Molly. "Just like Gran's."
But Molly's mum said she must wait to see if she liked the
classes before they bought any shoes.

For the dance class Molly and Beverly wore their prettiest dresses. "Hello, I'm Mrs Clover," said the teacher. "Welcome to our dance class." Molly looked at the teacher's shoes. They were silver. She looked around the hall. Nearly all the other girls had silver shoes, too.

"Mrs Clover, I haven't got any silver shoes,"
said Molly in dismay.
"That's okay," said the teacher, smiling.
"But my Gran has silver shoes for
dancing," said Molly in a wobbly voice.
She buried her head in her mum's dress.
"Mummy, I want to go home."

The following week, Beverly ran into Molly's house
holding a pair of shoes — silver shoes.
"Look what I have!" she shouted.

Beverly had been given an old pair of silver shoes that her cousin
had outgrown. Molly didn't want to play with her friend now.
But Mum had an idea.

At the charity shop, they found a blouse for Mum, two jigsaw puzzles, and some toys for Steven, but no silver shoes for Molly.

Then Molly saw them. A beautiful pair of silver shoes almost exactly the same as Gran's.

"Mummy, look, I've found them!" she shrieked.

"Those are adult shoes, Molly," said Mum. "You won't be able to dance in them." But Molly wanted them anyway.

Molly kept the silver shoes by her bed that night. As soon as she woke up, she put them on and she wore them all day long. She couldn't wait to show them to Gran.

Together they twirled
around Gran's tiny living room
until they were dizzy.

On Tuesday, Molly and Beverly went to dance class again.
"Look, Mrs Clover, I have my silver shoes now. They are just like
my Gran's and she does proper dancing," said Molly proudly.

But Mrs Clover shook her head.

"I'm sorry, Molly, high heels won't do," she said kindly.

"You might trip up and hurt yourself. Please, wear your ordinary shoes."

Daddy came home early that evening.
"Let's go to the park," he suggested.
"You can ride your bike, Molly."
"Yippee!" Molly cried. "I'll wear
my silver shoes."
Daddy looked at Mummy.
"Why don't you wear your other shoes
to ride your bike, Molly? You can
put the silver shoes in the basket."

Daddy pushed Molly and Steven high on the swings and bought them both an ice lolly.

They had such a good time that Molly forgot all about her silver shoes until bedtime.

Molly snuggled under the bedclothes as Daddy tucked her in.
"I'd really like some proper silver shoes," she sighed.
"Now Molly, I'll tell you a secret," whispered Dad. "Special
things that you want very much often come at special times."
"But I may have to wait ages for a special time," said Molly.
"Plenty of time then, pet, to learn some new dances with
Mrs Clover," replied Dad.
Molly smiled sleepily and hugged her daddy goodnight.

At dance class the next week, Molly was concentrating so hard she forgot she was wearing ordinary shoes. The following week, Molly had such fun she didn't think about her shoes at all.

And in the third week, she danced so fast she could hardly
see her feet!

In the fourth week, it was Molly's birthday. She tore open her presents one by one. She saved Gran and Grandad's present until last.

"Silver shoes! My own silver shoes!" cried Molly happily, and she put them on.

Now Molly felt like
a proper dancer.

But she still liked to wear her clickerty-clackerty shoes
when she danced for Gran.

MORE TITLES FROM FRANCES LINCOLN CHILDREN'S BOOKS

CHRISTY'S DREAM
Caroline Binch

Christy has wanted a pony for as long as he can remember. Lots of other boys
on the estate have their own horses, so now Christy's saved up enough money,
no-one can stop him making his dream come true. Except his ma.
What will she say when he brings his new horse home? Christy's passionate
determination to fulfil his dream, set against the realism of a Dublin
tower block estate, is perfectly evoked by Caroline Binch's
richly detailed illustrations.

ISBN 1-84507-472-6

PETAR'S SONG
Pratima Mitchell
Illustrated by Caroline Binch

Petar loves music, and the tunes he plays on his violin keep everyone
in the village dancing. But when war breaks out Petar, his mother, brother
and sister have to leave their valley and cross the border to safety,
leaving their father behind. Pratima Mitchell's story of the impact
of war and the pain caused by family separation, powerfully illustrated
by Caroline Binch, is full of hope for the future.

ISBN 0-7112-2078-6

GREGORY COOL
Caroline Binch

When a cool city boy meets the full warmth of the Caribbean,
anything can happen. Gregory is determined not to enjoy himself
when he is sent off to visit his grandparents in rural Tobago.
After a whole variety of adventures, however, he begins to think
that life outside the city may not be so bad after all.

ISBN 0-7112-0890-5

Frances Lincoln titles are available from all good bookshops.
You can also buy books and find out more about your favourite titles, authors and illustrators
on our website: www.franceslincoln.com